J.B.'s Christmas Presents

By **Evelyn Turman**

This book is dedicated to my husband,
Calvin Turman and family.

They have always encouraged me
in my endeavors.

J.B.'s Christmas Presents
Copyright © 2004 by Evelyn Turman
All rights reserved

Illustrated by Adam Turman

ISBN 0-9753042-0-8

Printing by Falcon Books

San Ramon, California

PRINTED IN THE UNITED STATES OF AMERICA

Joseph Benjamin Appleby, or J.B.
as he was called, was very sad.

The boys and girls at school had been
teasing him and calling him names.

It was true that
he couldn't run
as fast as some.

It was true that
he couldn't see
very well.

It was true he
stood back and
was chosen last
for all games.

But what was true most of all, that no one had noticed, was that J.B. felt very bad about all the taunts and name-calling.

"Oh, don't choose J.B.," called David.

"We don't want J.B. on our team," yelled Michael.

"J.B. can't catch a ball," shouted Sara.

Soon, the leaves fell from the trees, the days grew shorter, and the air outside turned cold.

So as Christmas
Eve approached,
J.B. went to bed
feeling miserable.
What he really
wanted most of
all for Christmas
were friends.

Meanwhile at the North Pole...

Santa was so busy getting ready to deliver presents that he forgot his stardust.

Stardust is magic and helps
Santa when he is in trouble.

The first stop on Santa's route
was J.B.'s house on the corner.

"Let's see, what do I have for
J.B.", said Santa. He left him a
sled, skates, games, and books.

Next, Santa went to Michael's house and down the chimney. Michael's chimney was smaller and Santa had put on a little weight.

"Oh dear me," said Santa halfway down.

"I'm stuck and cannot move. I'll use my stardust, but where is it?

The reindeer waited for Santa
to appear but no Santa came.

Finally they didn't know what to do.
"Let's go see Mrs. Claus," said Blitzen,
and away they flew to the North Pole.

Mrs. Claus saw the reindeer and realized that Santa had forgotten his stardust. She found it, jumped into the sleigh and the reindeer brought her back to Michael's house.

She sprinkled stardust down the chimney and Santa rose up to the top. It was early morning and too late for Santa to distribute any more presents.

Also, J.B.'s lights were on and Santa
couldn't retrieve those presents.

Then Santa and Mrs. Claus
flew back to the North Pole.

Christmas morning, J.B. saw his toys and
went outside to play in the snow with his sled.

David looked and could find no presents. Michael
looked and could find no toys. Sara looked and
could find no toys. All the children of Maples
Corners looked and could find no toys.

They
looked
outside and saw
J.B. playing with his
shiny red sled. J.B. called
and invited everyone to play with
the new toys Santa had left for him.

Meanwhile at
the North Pole,

Santa pondered and pondered.

Finally he said to Mrs. Claus, "I have only one choice, I'll deliver the rest tonight."

So he put in a note with the toys that said: "Dear Children,

Due to unforeseen circumstances, Christmas is a day late.

Sorry - Santa Claus"

The day after Christmas the rest of the children
received their toys and the note.

David wondered and wondered? Michael wondered
and wondered? Sara wondered and wondered? All the
children of Maples Corners wondered and wondered?

After Christmas, when J.B. started back to
school, there outside his door were Michael,
David, and Sara ready to walk with him.

J.B. received what he wanted most of
all for Christmas, many, many friends!

Tips on Enhancing Critical Thinking Skills

1. What do you think the children of Maples Corners thought when they saw only J.B. received presents from Santa Claus on Christmas Day?

2. How would you feel if you were J.B.?

3. Would you be happy that the other children received presents the day after Christmas?

4. If you were J.B. would you think this was a good Christmas? Why?

5. What do you think helped change David, Michael, and Sara's attitude toward J.B.?

6. Retell the story in your own words.